SMALL FOOT

Adapted by
Maggie Testa

Illustrated by
Masanori Hase

Meechee's Top
Secret Society

Simon Spotlight
New York London Toronto Sydney New Delhi

SIMON SPOTLIGHT
An imprint of Simon & Schuster Children's Publishing Division
1230 Avenue of the Americas, New York, New York 10020
This Simon Spotlight paperback edition August 2018
All rights reserved, including the right of reproduction in whole or in part in any form.
SIMON SPOTLIGHT and colophon are registered trademarks of Simon & Schuster, Inc.
For information about special discounts for bulk purchases, please contact Simon & Schuster Special Sales at 1-866-506-1949
or business@simonandschuster.com.
Manufactured in the United States of America 0718 LAK
10 9 8 7 6 5 4 3 2 1
ISBN 978-1-5344-3170-6
ISBN 978-1-5344-3171-3 (eBook)

Hello! We're so glad you could make it to our humble headquarters. I'm Meechee, leader of the Smallfoot Evidentiary Society, or S.E.S. for short. As you can see from the evidence we've gathered here in this cave, we believe that the legendary Smallfoot creature exists. Are you with us? Good. Then it's time for you to meet the other members of the group.

This is Kolka.

Kolka is our expert on Smallfoot artifacts. I'll let Kolka explain.

This is Gwangi.

Gwangi, just like the rest of the S.E.S., disagrees with the village law that says, "Smallfoot doesn't exist."

He also knows why the village leader, the Stonekeeper (and my dad), thinks that it's dangerous for the yetis to question the law. . . .

This is Fleem.

Fleem always says what he's thinking.
He might be little, but everyone in the
village knows he's got a big mouth.

The Smallfoot has got to be shorter than me, right?

And finally, this is our newest member, Migo.

Migo never questioned anything the Stonekeeper told him, until one day, he saw a Smallfoot with his very own eyes.

When he told everyone in the village, the Stonekeeper banished him.

All of us yetis needed to know the truth.

It was time for the S.E.S. to get some answers. And the only way to do that was to go down into the nothingness below the clouds.

Which is exactly what Migo did.

Poor Migo. It would have been a smooth trip, but my brother, Thorp, snuck up on us, and then Gwangi let go of Migo's rope because he was scared.

Thorp is very loyal to the Stonekeeper, so we had to keep what we were doing a secret from him.

Luckily for the S.E.S., and especially Migo, he landed without getting hurt. And there, in the nothingness below our village, Migo found something. Something wonderful. And he brought it back to us.

It. Was. A. Smallfoot!

We brought the Smallfoot to the village. All the Yetis were amazed. They were so curious!

The Smallfoot didn't speak the same language as us, but we did our best to communicate. He told me about his world. It was all so cool!

There was so much about Smallfoot that the S.E.S. didn't know.

But there was one Yeti who didn't welcome the Smallfoot—my dad, the Stonekeeper. He worried that the Smallfoot was dangerous. So he told the villagers that the Smallfoot was fake and it was just a hairless yak!

To make things worse, Migo decided to take the Stonekeeper's side. He told everyone that the S.E.S. was just a bunch of village weirdos! Can you believe it? Migo betrayed the S.E.S.!

Gwangi, Fleem, Kolka, and I were so angry. Migo had been an important member, and a friend, of the S.E.S.

But then Migo and my dad apologized. They had just wanted to keep the village safe from harm.

So that's the story of how the S.E.S. met its first Smallfoot and achieved our mission—proving the existence of Smallfoot. We should get a "best yeti society ever" award or something.

And I have good news for you—the S.E.S. is open to new members!

So what do you think? Do you want to join us on our next adventure?